3003600129432 9

A WORLD OF HOLIDAYS

Id-ul-Fitr

THE FARMINGTON COMMUNITY LIBRARY
FARMINGTON HILLS BRANCH
32737 West Twelve Mile Road
Farmington Hills, MI 48334-3302

W9-CNA-249

A WORLD OF HOLIDAYS

Id-ul-Fitr

Rosalind Kerven

RSVP
RAINTREE
STECK-VAUGHN
PUBLISHERS
The Steck-Vaughn Company

Austin, Texas

© Copyright 1997, text, Steck-Vaughn Company

All rights reserved. No part of this book may be reproduced or utilized in any form or by any means, electronic or mechanical, including photocopying, recording, or by any information storage and retrieval system, without permission in writing from the Publisher. Inquiries should be addressed to:
Copyright Permissions, Steck-Vaughn Company,
P.O. Box 26015, Austin, TX 78755

Published by Raintree Steck-Vaughn Publishers,
an imprint of Steck-Vaughn Company

Library of Congress Cataloging-in-Publication Data

Kerven, Rosalind.
    Id-ul-Fitr / Rosalind Kerven.
      p.   cm. — (A world of holidays)
    Includes bibliographical references (p.   ) and index.
    Summary: Introduces some of the beliefs and customs of Muslims, particularly those connected with the Great Festival of Id al-Fitr.
    ISBN 0-8172-4609-6
    1. Id al-Fitr—Juvenile literature.   2. Islam—Customs and practices—Juvenile literature.   [1. Fasts and feasts—Islam.   2. Islam—Customs and practices.]   I. Title.
II. Series.
BP186.45.K47   1997
297'. 36—dc20   96-42307
                                                                    CIP
                                                                    AC

Printed in Spain
Bound in United States
1 2 3 4 5 6 7 8 9 0   99 98 97 96

Acknowledgments

Editor: Su Swallow, Pam Wells
Design: Neil Sayer
Production: Jenny Mulvanny

The Author and Publishers would like to thank the Muslim Educational Trust for their help in the preparation of this book.

The author and publishers would like to thank the following for permission to reproduce photographs:

Title page: Trip
page 6 Trip **page 7** (top and bottom) Trip **page 8** Sarah Errington, Hutchison Library **page 9** Trip **page 10** Circa Photo Library **page 11** Axiom/Jim Holmes **page 12** Axiom/Jim Holmes **page 13** Trip **page 14** Circa Photo Library **page 15** (top) Carlos Freire, Hutchison Library (bottom) Trip **page 16** John Miles/Panos Pictures **page 17** Trip **page 18** Trip **page 19** Trip **page 20** Trip **page 21** Circa Photo Library **page 22** Trip **page 23** (top and bottom) Trip **page 24** Trip **page 25** Trip **page 26** Circa Photo Library **page 27** (top and bottom) Trip

Contents

No Food, No Fighting

Wake up! The new day is breaking, and a bright lamp is burning in the minaret of the local mosque. It's the first day of Ramadan, the Muslim holy month. This is when most adults and many older children "fast," or go without any food or drink, from dawn until sunset.

Everyone has an early breakfast. Then gradually the sky gets lighter. The Koran, the Muslim holy book, says that fasting must begin with the white threads barely seen at the breaking of dawn.

A TIME TO THINK

Fasting is very difficult and uncomfortable, but it reminds Muslims how lucky they are to have enough to eat and drink the rest of the time. It makes them think of the world's poor people who never have enough food or clean water.

This restaurant in Tunisia is closed every day during Ramadan.

Whenever they feel hungry or thirsty during Ramadan, Muslims try to think of good deeds they could do to say "thank you" to God for all the happy things in life.

EVERYONE'S TOGETHER

In a Muslim community or country, everyone fasts together during Ramadan. Fasting together helps to create a good feeling of friendliness. People also try not to argue or to be angry during Ramadan.

As the sun sets, it's time for *iftar*, the evening meal. This usually starts with something light, such as dates or apricots soaked in sweetened water, or perhaps a special drink of sweetened, spicy milk. After that,

everyone can eat and drink as much as they need during the hours of darkness.

Ramadan cakes on sale.

The evening meal tastes especially good after a day of fasting!

✤ How It All Began ✤

About 1,400 years ago, a man called Muhammad lived in the city of Mecca, now in modern Saudi Arabia. He became the Prophet of God. During Ramadan, young Muslims often listen to this story of his life.

Muslim children in Kyrgystan, in Central Asia, reading the Koran. Like all Muslim children, they learn to read the Koran in Arabic, even though Arabic is not their own language.

8

THE FIRST MUSLIMS

Muhammad was very upset by all the poverty, cruelty, and violence he saw in the world. To escape from it, he used to go off into the desert on his own for long periods, to think.

One day while he was alone in a desert cave in a hilly area, he suddenly saw a vision of the Angel Jibril (Gabriel) and heard a voice saying,

"Recite! In the name of thy Lord who has created everything, who has created Man from a clot of blood."

At first, Muhammad was afraid. He went home and talked about this vision with his wife, Khadijah. With her support, he soon realized that it really was a direct message from God.

Muhammad received many more messages through the Angel Jibril over the next 23 years. Many were about God. They also explained all the rules for living a good life.

Soon Muhammad began to obey the angel's command to "recite." He started to repeat these messages to other people, who became his followers. They were the first Muslims. Muhammad was their Prophet, and this was how the religion of Islam began.

Muslims come from all over the world to pray in the Great Mosque in Mecca. They all face the Ka'bah, the stone monument in the middle.

A Very Special Book

Like most people of his time, Muhammad could not read or write, but his messages were carefully remembered and repeated by special

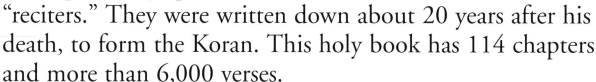

Copies of the Koran are often beautifully decorated, to show that it is a very special, holy book.

"reciters." They were written down about 20 years after his death, to form the Koran. This holy book has 114 chapters and more than 6,000 verses.

PRECIOUS AND BEAUTIFUL
The Koran is usually kept carefully wrapped up in a safe place. When someone reads aloud from it, everyone listens quietly.

The Koran is written in Arabic. This is the language Muhammad spoke to his people. The Koran has been translated into most of the world's different languages, but Muslims in every country still try to learn it by heart in Arabic.

THE FIVE PILLARS
Muslims try very hard to live by the rules laid down in the Koran. They believe that God made these rules to show people how to live happily together. The most important rules are known as the "Five Pillars" of Islam. One of these is fasting during Ramadan. The others are belief in God, regular daily prayers, giving to charity, and making a pilgrimage to the holy city of Mecca.

Arabic script on the wall of a mosque.

A girl in Pakistan uses a special book rest to hold the Koran.

11

Waiting for the New Moon

Muslims have their own special calendar. It is a "lunar" calendar, based on the cycles of the moon. The Muslim year is about 11 days shorter than years based on Western, or modern, calendars. The exact date of Ramadan changes every year. In 1995 it started on January 31. In 2010 it will probably begin on August 11.

Muslim women shopping, in preparation for the festivities to come.

WATCHING AND WAITING

By the 29th day of Ramadan everyone is wondering when the new moon will appear in the sky. This will signal the complete end of fasting and the start of a very happy festival. In some years, the moon does not appear until the 30th day, which means a whole extra day of fasting!

On the last night, many people stay up late for hours, excitedly watching and waiting for the moon. This can be very frustrating in countries where the weather is often bad, because sometimes the whole sky is covered by clouds. Today, the time of the new moon is worked out using scientific tools. Some family members who live in different parts of the world may call one another, as they begin to celebrate the Id-ul-Fitr.

At last—there it is! The hardship of Ramadan has been successfully completed. Now it is the first day of the new month, Shawwal, and time to celebrate the festival of Id-ul-Fitr. In countries where most people are Muslims, this usually marks the beginning of an official public holiday, with no school or work for at least two days.

12

The moon above a mosque in Dubai, in the United Arab Emirates. When the new moon appears, Ramadan will be over, and the happy festival of Id-ul-Fitr can begin.

Something for Everyone

As Ramadan comes to an end, everyone makes a special small payment to charity, known as *Zakat-ul-Fitr*. This is usually enough money to buy one adult's meals for one day. This amount is given for each person in the giver's family. It is collected together and given to a charity. The charity uses the money to prepare food for poor Muslims who cannot afford enough food to enjoy Id-ul-Fitr.

HAPPY TO PAY

In addition to this special collection, practicing Muslims pay another type of *zakat* once a year, every year. It is used to help the poor and needy. Islam teaches that everyone is equal in God's eyes, so that rich people should help poor people. Paying *zakat* is one of the Five Pillars of Islam. It is an important duty, and everyone is happy to pay it. There are special rules that tell how much each person should pay, depending on how rich they are.

Zakat helps people who cannot earn enough money for themselves. It is also used for homeless people, orphans, prisoners, travelers in need, and people who are studying Islam. Nobody feels too proud or ashamed to receive it, for the Koran teaches that all wealth really belongs to God anyway, so it should be shared fairly.

Muslims are always very happy to give zakat. The money collected goes to help other Muslims who are poor and in need.

14

Zakat may be used to help people who are studying Islam. These children are learning the Koran in India.

Old Islamic coins.

15

Fine Clothes, Fancy Patterns

On the morning of Id-ul-Fitr, the whole family gets up early. Everyone has a bath or shower, and then dresses up in their best clothes. The luckiest ones have brand new clothes especially for Id!

Many Muslims follow careful religious rules when choosing what to wear. They select long, loose, simple clothes, and women often wear a scarf over their hair. Islam teaches that women and girls should cover their whole bodies apart from the face and hands, while men and boys must be covered at least between the waist and the knees. Some people manage to fit these rules very well into the fashions of their country.

ALL THE TRIMMINGS

A special perfume is often worn by both women and men at Id. This tradition was started by the prophet Muhammad, who founded the Muslim religion. (See pages 8 and 9.)

Girls and women often decorate their hands with reddish brown *mehndi* patterns. These might look like trailing flowers and leaves, or simply twirling, abstract shapes. The color is made from dried henna leaves that are ground into a powder and mixed with a little lemon juice and water. Then this color is painted on with a toothpick.

When everyone is ready, it's time for early morning prayers, and then a light breakfast snack, perhaps of sweets and dates.

Women paint patterns on their hands for special occasions like weddings or some holidays.

16

Muslims wear their best clothes for Id. Like most Muslim women and girls, this girl is careful to cover her hair.

Hurry to the Mosque!

After breakfast it is time to go out to the mosque, the Muslim place of worship. There is always an enormous crowd there at Id. In some places there are so many people that the service overflows outside the main building. In hot countries, Id prayers may be held in a special place like a large park or even a field.

Inside a busy mosque in Cairo, Egypt, at Id.

As everyone hurries through the streets, they can hear the muezzin calling them. He stands in the minaret, or tower, of the mosque crying in Arabic, "God is the greatest! ... Come to prayer!" He might use a loudspeaker to make sure he can be heard a long way off.

On entering the mosque, each person stops to wash in the special room, or at the fountain. Then each one goes into the prayer hall. The women and girls use a separate area from the men and boys. There are no chairs or seats in there, but there are carpets. The walls may be beautifully decorated with patterns and special Arabic calligraphy or writing.

PRAYERS AND PEACE

At last the muezzin calls out, "Come to pray! Come to success!" The imam (prayer leader) takes his place in the minbar (pulpit), and the service begins. Everyone joins in special Id prayers to say "thank you" to God, and to ask for help to live a good life and obey all the laws of Islam. After

A mosque in Uzbekistan, in Central Asia, is overflowing with worshipers, so some people have to pray outside.

prayers are finished, each person turns toward his or her neighbor saying "Salaam" or "Peace be upon you." Then they listen as the imam gives a special talk, perhaps about helping other people through charity. Muslims always try to celebrate festivals in a way that will please God.

Then worshipers pour out of the mosque to greet their relations and friends. There are lots of happy smiles and hugs! The children are especially excited as they admire each other's new clothes.

Colorful Cards

In the weeks leading up to Id, the local shops have been full of special greetings cards. Some mosques set up their own stands, selling cards and other festive items. Children often prefer to make their own! Soon every home has a fine display of Id cards received from relations and friends.

PATTERNS, NOT PICTURES
The front of an Id card usually has a beautiful pattern of flowers, leaves, vines, stars, or intricate shapes and twirling lines. Sometimes it might show a garden, a mosque, a pattern of decorated arches, or a design of stars and the moon. However, you will never see pictures of people or animals in a mosque or on an Id card. Muslims believe that if an artist draws or paints a living creature, he or she will be punished for trying to copy God's unique powers of creation.

Children at a mosque proudly display their homemade Id cards.

20

WRITING AS ART

Id cards are often brightly colored. Blue and gold are especially popular. They symbolize heaven and the sun.

Inside the card, there is usually a special greeting, such as "Best wishes for the Happy Id" or "Wishing you the blessings of Id." This greeting is often written in Arabic, followed by English or another local language.

Arabic has a completely different alphabet from English. It is written from right to left, so that Id cards are folded on the right-hand side. The Arabic message is often written in beautiful, sweeping strokes.

Decorated Id cards.

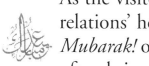

﷽ A Family Feast ﷽

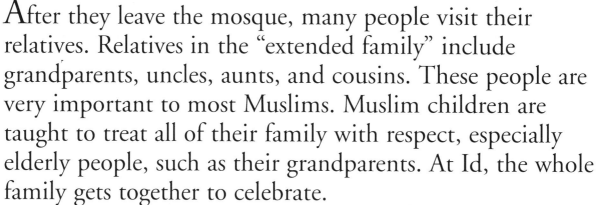

After they leave the mosque, many people visit their relatives. Relatives in the "extended family" include grandparents, uncles, aunts, and cousins. These people are very important to most Muslims. Muslim children are taught to treat all of their family with respect, especially elderly people, such as their grandparents. At Id, the whole family gets together to celebrate.

"HOPE YOU'RE HUNGRY!"

As the visitors arrive at their relations' house, people call out *Id Mubarak!* or "Happy festival!" They often bring presents, such as gift-wrapped cakes or dried fruits, such as apricots, figs, or raisins, and money for the children.

About midday, the whole family sits down to enjoy a special meal for the Id.

These children are holding a special Id's treat.

EAT WELL

Muslims try to prepare their best dishes for the guests on Id day. The women do most of the cooking, but some men like to help in the kitchen on Id day. There is no special food for Id—it depends on where the people live. In India, Muslims might eat a delicious Id pudding made of rice or fine pasta. It is sweet and spicy and very filling. Muslims do not eat pork, but they eat other kinds of meats. The animals must be killed in a special way. Muslims do not drink alcohol. On festival days they like to drink something sweet and refreshing.

Some people have many houses to visit at Id, and they will be given something to eat at each one!

A stand selling dried fruits in Morocco. People give dried fruits as presents at Id.

Eating is an important part of Id celebrations.

23

 Fun and Fairs

After the meal is over, there is often a party for the "extended family." In some Muslim countries there are special fairs, parades, and entertainments.

Id is a good time for family outings. Some people like to visit famous buildings or watch dancers and listen to music. The performers might dress up in their national costumes.

Other people make their own music and join in the dancing. Children like to try out all the rides at the amusement park.

The paintings of Id are by Muslim children. The painting above shows an Id fair in Turkey. The painting on the left shows men dancing with swords to drum music.

▶ Dancing in the park in Cairo, Egypt, during Id.

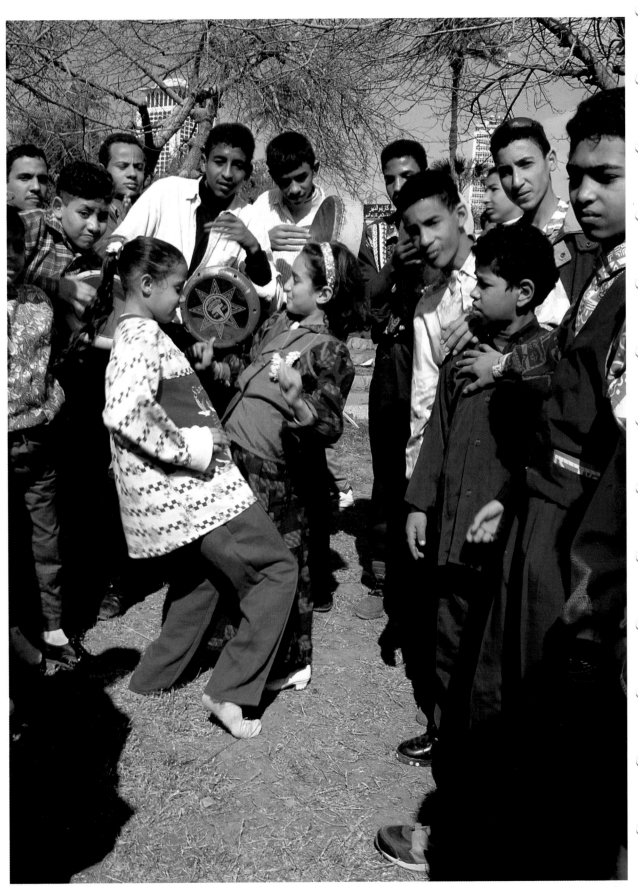

# Thank You for a Lovely Day!

It has been a very long, exciting, and happy day. Now it's time to go to bed. But good Muslim children, like their parents, would not dream of doing this until they have said their prayers.

A father and son pray at home.

Muslims pray five times a day. The first prayers are said before sunrise. The other prayer times are midday, midafternoon, after sunset, and before bedtime. Because they pray so often, Muslims never forget the importance of God in their lives.

AN EVERYDAY CEREMONY

The best place to pray is in a mosque, but, of course, this is not possible for most people, most of the time. So Muslims are used to praying at home, at school, at work—or wherever they happen to be.

A prayer compass shows which way to face Mecca.

    Before praying, Muslims always have to prepare by washing. Then they turn to face the holy city of Mecca. (See pages 9 and 10.) Many people have a special compass to show the right direction.

BEAUTIFUL MATS

Muslims pray using special movements. They stand, hold up their hands, cross them over the waist, bow, then kneel and touch the floor with their nose and forehead.

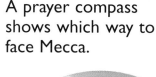

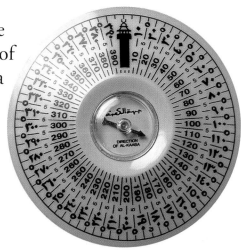

Because they have to kneel and touch the floor, most people roll out prayer mats to make it more comfortable. These are often decorated with Islamic patterns. Some prayer mats are really beautiful and thickly woven.

SPECIAL THOUGHTS

After saying the set prayers in Arabic, people usually add a special private prayer of their own, in their own language. You can guess what most children will be adding tonight. They will be saying thank you for all the food, presents, and fun they have had this Id-ul-Fitr.

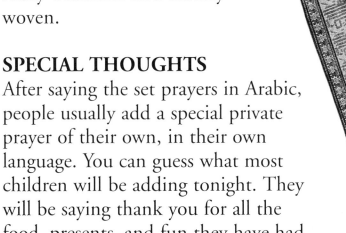

Many people own beautifully decorated prayer mats.

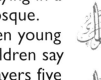

Let's Celebrate!

MAKE AN ID PUDDING

Things you will need:

- measuring cup
- teaspoon
- large spoon for stirring
- saucepan
- serving dish ($^1/_2$-quart-size)
- 2 cups vermicelli, broken into small pieces
- $^1/_2$ cup margarine
- 2 cups water
- $^1/_4$ cup sugar
- $^1/_4$ cup raisins
- $^1/_4$ cup flaked almonds
- $^1/_4$ teaspoon vanilla
- 2 glacé cherries (cut in half)

Directions:

1. Find an adult to help you.
2. Wash your hands.
3. Put the broken vermicelli into the saucepan with the water.
4. Bring it to a boil, then turn the heat down.
5. Stir the vermicelli occasionally to keep it from sticking to the pan.
6. Continue cooking on a low heat until all the water has evaporated (about 8 minutes).
7. Remove the saucepan from the heat.
8. Add margarine, sugar, vanilla, almonds, and raisins to the vermicelli.
9. Stir until the margarine has melted, and all the ingredients are well mixed.
10. Turn into the serving dish.
11. Smooth the top and decorate with glacé cherries.

MAKE AN ID CARD

Materials:

- one sheet of stiff paper or cardboard
- paints, colored pencils, or felt-tipped pens

Directions:

1. Fold the cardboard. Remember to keep the fold on the righthand side!
2. Choose one of these ideas to draw:

  flowers and leaves

  a garden

  stars and the moon

  a mosque or part of a mosque

3. Draw it on the front of the card. (Do not draw any animals, birds, or people.)
4. Color it in brightly. Try to make it look beautiful.

5. Copy this piece of Arabic writing inside, on the lefthand side.
6. Underneath write "Best wishes for the Happy Id." Try to make your writing beautiful and decorative.

Glossary

Arabic The language spoken in Arabia, much of North Africa, and the Middle East. Also the holy language of Islam.

Calligraphy Beautiful handwriting.

Charity Giving money to those in need.

Community A group of people living in one area.

Fast, fasting Going without food for religious reasons.

Imam Muslim leader and teacher.

Islam The Muslim religion.

Koran The holy book of Islam.

Mosque Muslim place of worship.

Muezzin Muslim who calls people to prayer at the mosque.

Muslim Someone who believes in the religion of Islam.

Prophet A special religious teacher who explains God's will to the people.

Further Reading

Ahmad, Fazl. *Some Companions of the Prophet.* Kazi, 1985.

Bakhtiar, Laleh. *We Are Muslim Children.* American Trust Publications, 1993.

Hamid, J. *Islamic Activity Books I-III.* Kazi, 1988.

Iqbal, Muhammad. *Way of the Muslim.* Dufour, 1983.

MacMillan, Dianne M. *Ramadan and Id al-Fitr* (Best Holiday Books series). Dufour, 1983.

FICTION

Kezzeiz, Ediba. *Ramadan Adventures of Fasfoose Mouse.* American Trust, 1991.

Index

© Copyright Evans Brothers Limited 1996